# GUILTY OR NOT...?

## SECRETS OF A WANTED CRIMINAL

DRISH KING

Made with ♥ on the Notion Press Platform
www.notionpress.com

To my mother, Dr.Sonia Kochhar, for allowing me to pursue my dreams along with my studies...

# Contents


*Preface* *vii*

*Prologue* *ix*

1. Henry Spark's Demise 1

2. Speculating The Clues 6

3. The Big Lead 11

4. The Unnecessary Spice 16

5. Investigation Takes A Turn 21

6. Soovin And Hannah's Face-Off 26

7. Breaking Leads To Building 31

8. An Amusing Call 36

9. Duty Or Emotions...? 41

10. Overcoming Dead Ends 46

11. Soovin Makes A Mistake 52

12. A Magical Connection 58

5 Years Later 65

About The Author 69

Books By The Author 71

# Preface

I have a million worlds and characters trapped inside my mind—all fighting to get a voice on paper. Being a high schooler, it gets very hectic at times to balance studying and following my dreams. Still, I somehow always manage to squeeze some time for reading and writing, my two favorite things on the entire planet.

For me, at this point, reading is breathing in and writing is breathing out. I can't prevail without either of them. Writing is my way to express myself, my emotions, and my intellect. What started as a hobby has now become a burning passion.

I personally love writing crime. However, that creates severe competition when it comes to publishing them. This is my first book with crime as a genre that has been published as a paperback along with an ebook.

I have written ebooks on crime but they always fail to touch the world limit. I get easily bored and writing mundane scenarios is just a headache for me. I prefer short stories in crime, to never break the suspense and mystery for even a second. That way, even the writer along with the reader is hooked and has to fight himself to put the laptop down as the readers struggle to put the book down.

Somehow, I have managed to extend this story without making it mundane and I am pretty proud of this accomplishment. So, here I am, presenting you my book 'Guilty Or Not...? - The Secrets Of A Wanted Criminal'

I have put a lot of effort into it and I hope you find this story worth your time. Though I have tried to increase its length, it's still a novella, just a quick read you can go through if you are bored on a Sunday.

But don't judge it by its length. Beware, dear reader. I have spiked every chapter, every page with twists and turns, hidden mysteries and clues, traumatic pasts, contradictions, emotions crossing paths with duty, and enormous character development.

So, if you are looking for a roller-coaster read that will have you cry your eyes out, give you a stomach ache from laughing too hard, and a headache from mysteries and anticipation, you have picked the correct book, buddy.

Join me as I introduce you to a world filled with chaos.

# Prologue

It was a normal and peaceful night for everyone but the last for Henry Spark. He was sitting alone and talking over the phone with his brother.

"Is Anna good?" He asked about his daughter.

"She is watching cartoons while chuckling. I will take that as a yes" A laugh erupted from the other side of the phone.

Henry shook his head at his brother's peculiar sense of humor.

"I am feeling weird today" He admitted after a while, making the conversation drift from random talks to serious ones.

"Why? Is everything good?" Concern was dripping from his brother's voice.

"Yes...I just...I don't know, man. I am feeling a sense of...finality...as if my purpose in life is over..."

"And what will that purpose be?" Henry could almost see his brother's eyebrows raise in question.

"To drink at the club until you pass out?" Henry said in an attempt to dissolve the tension building between them.

They both laughed.

Henry's brother's laugh was genuine but Henry was just trying to mask his apparent fear and sudden uneasiness as if...someone was eyeing him.

He continued to glance back and forth but his eyes found nothing.

He made himself comfortable on the couch, trying to shake off the strange feeling he had never experienced before.

"See you later, buddy!"

As soon as he cut the call, he shivered from head to toe upon hearing someone thumping at his door.

"WHO IS IT?!" He shouted.

Instead of a reply, Henry was greeted with an even more violent thump.

But before he could do anything else, an unknown hooded person managed to enter the room by force. The mysterious man swiftly bolted the door and came toward Henry whose face was pale with pure fright.

Soon, the street was filled with ear-piercing screams. All the neighborhood lights were switched on. The neighbors came out of their houses. They panicked on hearing more cries and then, a window shattering.

It was then, that they decided to call the police. But it was too late for Henry...

Mr. Dune leaned in his chair and smoked his pipe. His CIA badge was glistening while his eyes were focused on the case file of Henry Spark sitting in front of him.

He flipped the page.

His pipe fell from his mouth in shock as he glanced at the list of suspicious people spotted near the crime scene. There were twelve or so names but his eyes were focused on only one of them.

He snapped the file shut and said to himself, "I know just the officer for this case"

He immediately called an officer and instructed him, "Assign this case to Officer Hannah Gorgin"

The officer took the file but said uncertainly, "Sir...forbid me for questioning but...she is one of our best agents and this...seems to be a rather low-profile case"

Mr. Dune just smiled and whispered under his breath, "Oh, this is going to be fun..." as he continued smoking his pipe.

CHAPTER ONE

# Henry Spark's Demise

I sighed heavily as I studied the crime scene before me. A white outline was indicating the dead body in the cluttered room of Henry Spark. The cops were gabbing loudly about the murder. A glare from me does the job as silence unfurls.

The numerous badges beside my CIA ID, 'Hannah Gorgin' were enough for them to be compliant with me and terrified of my icy look. My hard reputation and firm principles were just the icing on the art.

The victim's family was standing together, outside the house. In such cases of murder of a middle-class man, his family was always the number one suspect. My seven years of experience were screaming inside my head to interrogate them and get this cakewalk of a case over with.

Boy, I had never been more wrong...

I tried to connect the dots for the billionth time. This was the first time Mr.Dune had transferred such a low-profile case to me. When I confronted him regarding it, he said that an *interesting* personality was spotted near the crime scene. The one and only criminal I had attempted to catch and failed. The only criminal whose file I had failed to close in my years of service.

Mr.Dune was pretty confident that *he* was involved in this but I felt it was pretty unlikely because he performed only the impossible. Killing a normal citizen was something well below his level.

It sounded rather ridiculous that the most wanted assassin of all time, Soovin Cooper had killed a middle-class innocent man in the easiest and quickest way possible and then, quietly made his escape without leaving any mark behind, symbolizing his never-ending criminal legacy and the CIA's failure at stopping him. I was not at all willing to buy it.

Nonetheless, I had devoted my mind to this case. I couldn't remember the last time Mr. Dune had been proved wrong. That guy's speculations were as accurate as if he had stolen them from fate itself. If even the slightest chance of the speculated involvement was true, the tables could turn. The CIA could finally put Soovin behind bars for the good.

I glanced at Henry Spark's family through the open door.

His brother was crying with his wife. The tears seemed genuine but one can never be sure these days. Property, money, rivalry, the reasons were endless. Henry's mother was weeping loud enough to wake the dead while Henry's father tried to calm her in vain.

Henry's little daughter, however, wasn't crying or showing any readable emotion. I frowned at first. My brows eased when I realized that perhaps she was dumbfounded. Maybe she was too small to understand what had happened to her beloved dad or he would never return.

Life had taken away both her parents from her at a tender age. The reports said that her mother had died due to cancer shortly after her birth and now her father was gone as well. That poor soul had already seen Life's ruthless and stone-hearted side. She had already endured more scars than what time could heal.

I watered down my feelings and analyzed the room, allowing my professional side to take control over me. Fallen books, blood stains on the wall, a strand of hair matching Henry's profile, and a night lamp lying broken on the floor. One of the mosaic tiles was smashed.

I bent to take a closer look at it and scrutinized the black marks and smudges, caressing them with my gloved thumb.

A gunshot was my immediate thought.

Air came in from the broken window, moving the sheet covering the dead body of Henry Spark. The victim's face was filled with bruises. His eyes revealed utter fear and his neck had red markings on it, roughly forming a right hand.

*A right hand,* I started jotting down the clues that could lead me to Soovin in my mind.

A bullet was in the center of Henry's forehead, another in his chest and yet another was lying on the floor.

I adjusted my gloves and cautiously picked up the bullet to examine it. A smile crept on my lips as I felt a tinge of hope inside my chest. The bullet was all too familiar. A Canik 55 TP9 handgun was just his choice. It was the same gun he had used before.

After all, the similarities were more than I had anticipated at first.

A thrill surged through my body. Maybe Mr.Dune was right. Maybe heindeed had a hand in it. Just maybe...I could get my hands on him this time.

I smirked in triumph and merrily thought, *Soovin Cooper, here I come...*

With sheer determination and a newly found dedication, I opened my eyes and looked around almost desperately, anxious to absorb every little detail, frantic to search for every possible mistake he could have made. My fingers ached to investigate every nook and cranny till I found something, anything that could lead me to him.

It took me ages but after I had imprinted every little detail in my brain, I closed my eyes.

My mind was racing with possibilities. My neurons were overloaded with details. It seemed as if I was processing the clues, and crafting from them, the murder scene itself.

It was an ability my experience had taught me over a span of seven years.

I took a deep breath, exhaling slowly. I opened my eyes as the murder scene played in front of me.

A six-foot-tall, masculine figure broke into the room while the victim was sitting on the couch and bolted the door.

The mysterious man punched him in the face, giving him a black eye. Henry fell and got up to oppose but the killer hurled him down again. The merciless being grabbed his hair and callously dragged him to the corner of the room. He kicked him hard in the stomach. Henry spat out blood, painting the carpet red. The killer picked him up and dragged him ruthlessly against the bookshelf. Several books fell in protest. The cold-hearted being threw him at the wall and punched him repeatedly, loaded with unexplained anger and a touch of disgust.

Henry begged for his life and hugged the killer's feet, barely conscious and in need of immediate medical help. But the killer was barely humane and didn't know any emotion for he pinned Henry to the wall and held him high by the neck. Henry helplessly waved his hands and legs but he didn't let him go until his soul left his body.

As the lifeless body of Henry Sparks fell to the ground, he took out his Canik 55 TP9 handgun and shot at his forehead, then, his chest. Unable to control himself, he turned around and shot at the floor with flames of rage rising inside him.

He picked up the night lamp and studied it for a bit, contemplating his next move within seconds. He used it to break the window, making broken pieces of glass go flying around the room and then, smashed the night lamp onto the floor. After that, he jumped out of the window, evacuating the crime scene as if he had merely squashed a mosquito between his hands.

I jerked back to reality as I felt someone's hand on my shoulder.

## CHAPTER TWO

# SPECULATING THE CLUES

My heartbeat relaxed on seeing the familiar face of my brother, Frank Gorgin.

I could see myself in his blue eyes, that were identical to mine if you overlooked the spark of mischief in them. His eyebrows were arched, probably after seeing me alone, imagining the entire murder like a lunatic. His blonde hair was messed up as usual.

"I heard you needed my assistance to go home, little girl. You are just as useless as the day Mum picked you up from the trash can"

I looked at the watch, "Time flies...Also, are you talking about that very trash can beside the orphanage that used to be your home?"

"Falsehoods. Also, I am not the one who does a perilous job and ends up losing her own car to a criminal"

"You know there are almost seven trillion nerves in a human body and you manage to step on EVERY SINGLE ONE OF THEM!"

That was a sore spot. At the root of this incident was no one other than Soovin Cooper. In my previous case, when

I had nearly caught him, he had escaped by stealing *my* car. The humiliation and anger still made my blood boil.

This unfortunate event was the only reason I had to count on Frank to go around. I still felt the need to seek revenge against Soovin for what he did.

"You have nerves? Well, that's nice. Now, all that's missing is a brain and a feeling of gratitude. Then, you can proudly call yourself a human-"

He abruptly shut his eyes when his wandering gaze approached the dead body. I smiled. He had been preparing to join the CIA, following in my footsteps. After failing the exam a billion times, he decided to become an engineer instead, but, his dream of investigating crimes was still stirring inside him. However, he had no experience and therefore, seeing dead bodies made him uneasy.

"Well, at least I have the guts to see a dead body," I smirked at him.

"Shut up, Han! Hurry if you don't want to get home by bus"

"Whatever blondie..." I muttered as I advanced toward Henry's lifeless body.

I covered it and punched his arm playfully, earning a scowl.

"Come on, now. I have to get home"

"Sure, idiot. Also, you owe me lunch for this service"

"Whatever pleases your soul..." I muttered as we went outside toward the car.

On my way, I came across one of the officers who stopped to talk to me.

She greeted me with a salute, "Good afternoon ma'am"

"Afternoon, officer. What brings you here?" I asked.

"Mr. Dune has sent the file of this case for you," she outstretched her hand holding the file.

"I am her brother, by the way," Frank interrupted us, clearly demanding attention.

She gave him a weird skeptical look.

"My name is Fra-"

"Just ignore him, please," I said with a smile tugging at my lips as Frank's gaze intended to burn a hole through my skull.

She smiled and nodded at me.

I took the file, "Thank you, officer. Give the old man my greetings"

"It will be my pleasure, ma'am," She left.

Frank opened his mouth to say something but I silenced him, "Not. A. Word."

"Whatever..." I heard him mutter under his breath as we advanced toward the car.

Our journey commenced as we got into the car and started our engine. The road was clear, and we cruised towards our destination with ease. After thirty minutes of driving, we finally arrived at our humble abode, feeling content and satisfied with our smooth and uneventful journey.

Upon arriving at the table, I made the decision to order a pizza that could be enjoyed by both of us. Taking into consideration our shared preferences, I requested a suitable option that would satisfy our taste buds and leave us feeling content.

Then, I opened the case file to figure out the mystery that had been bothering me for an hour.

"You always have your nose in some case file even when you don't have a brain" Frank mocked.

"Really? You solve it then, Mr. Didn't-even-pass-the-exam"

"I just lack experience and technology, that's all! Otherwise, I can solve it under-"

"Fine then. Show your extraordinary skills, Mr. Frank. You have access to my laptop and my help, if I feel like it"

"I don't want to waste my time"

"10 bucks on the line!"

"Oh, It's on! Han, keep the 10 bucks ready"

He studied the case file with me as I supplied details about the case I had noted on the crime scene.

I could see him trying his best, pushing his pea-sized brain's limits.

He thought for a horribly long while. Even when the pizza arrived, he was still scratching his head in hope that the solution would pop out of his brain.

As he savored the mouthwatering flavors of the cheesy pizza, his mind struggled to stay fixated on the current task and solve the formidable mystery he had earlier thought of as a piece of cake.

"The lamp was *half crushed,*" I gave him the most obvious hint yet his thick brain couldn't get it right.

He finally said, "If the night lamp wasn't completely crushed, then, maybe it has the fingerprints of the killer...?"

I smiled at him, "It's about time, idiot. That's what I am hoping for. But if the killer is smart, which he most probably is, he would have taken care of that"

"Then how will you find him...or her?"

I took a deep breath and began, "The house has CCTV footage. The neighbors might have seen something. Henry's postmortem might reveal something about the killer. His house is being searched thoroughly for more clues. Lastly, the bullet can be traced back to the gun, then, to the supplier, and then, finally, to the killer"

"Damn..."

"Still, I have got a feeling that we will barely get anywhere"

*Like the rest of the cases revolving around Soovin Cooper*, I thought bitterly.

"Really? Even with ALL these?"

"The killer has probably already taken care of nearly half of the clues. Judging by our suspects, he is probably a genius. I can bet that the gun has been bought secretly via the darknet and is hence, untraceable. Although our officers have interrogated half of the neighbours, they have barely gotten anywhere. There is no guarantee that-"

Suddenly, my phone rang.

CHAPTER THREE

# The Big Lead

I picked it up, "Hello, Hannah Gorgin speaking"

"Good Afternoon, ma'am," I recognized a somehow familiar, officer's voice from the other side of the line, "The reports of your new case, the postmortem of Henry Spark, to be precise, have arrived. Would you prefer them to be kept in your cabin or sent to your home?"

"I am coming to the headquarters. It would be kind of you to keep them in my cabin. Thank you"

"My pleasure, ma'am"

The call ended.

I turned to find Frank leaning over me so as to eavesdrop on my conversation.

I exclaimed, "FRANK! What-"

"Can I come too?"

I was taken aback by his spontaneous request.

"Why?" I scowled, quickly overcoming my surprise.

"Come on! You know it was my dream to investigate crime. I couldn't pass that exam but I still want to at least experience what it feels like to investigate a case. Please...?" Frank asked me with his pleading puppy eyes.

"I am not allowed to do that and you know it," I replied sternly.

"Given your reputation, even if you do it, no one has the guts to question Officer Hannah Gorgin and *you* know it," He shot back.

"It's about time that you act a bit mature. It's not a child's play, Frank. It's dangerous! You can't just simply tag along-"

"As dangerous as Mom when she gets to know *something...?*" He gave me a lopsided smirk.

I frowned and held my ground, "What do you mean?"

"I mean that...mom doesn't know that you went to a party on Saturday night and not to Marge's house for dinner...yet. If you wish for it to remain that way and not face Mom's wrath, then..."

"You manipulative, back-stabbing little-"

"I'll take that as a yes"

I sighed in defeat, swallowing all the words I wanted to yell at him.

"Eat fast if you don't want to stay home", I said while finishing the last slice of my appetizing pizza.

"Someone seems to forget who is gonna drive..." He muttered.

I clenched my jaw and gave him a death glare which silenced him quite effectively.

Within an hour, I found myself leaning in my cabin chair, sitting across Frank, and looking at the reports.

The red marks or handprints on Henry's neck had found a match in the database. A smile crept across my lips as I glanced at the name Soovin Cooper flashing across the screen in green color. I sighed with satisfaction. Now, I just had to scrutinize the crime scene for the slightest of clues and I would have him by his neck.

"Soovin Cooper...Who even is he?" Frank asked.

"Of course, you don't know about the most wanted assassin. His most recent deed was killing an influential leader last week. In a crowd of thousands, he shot at his heart. The reckless daredevil's crimes are smooth as butter"

"In the news, they implied the leader died of a heart attack"

"We can't just go around telling people that a man shot him despite his ultra-elevated security. Many people would have raised their fingers at us and let me tell you, it's not a pleasant experience"

"You guys still haven't caught him?"

My expression made him backtrack quickly, "I mean, no offense to your department *or you.* I am just asking due to...umm...curiosity"

I sighed, "He had scarcely left any clues. We could only find his profile in the database and confirm that he was the one behind the killing before he went underground...Why would he come out premature to kill an ordinary citizen?" I wondered.

"You said he was blinded by rage and had concealed anger. Can be a personal rivalry," Frank said, earning an impressed look. Now, that didn't happen every day.

"I just ran a check through the database. Nothing links Henry to Soovin except the fingerprints. However, him being in a fit of anger is a good sign for us. There is a possibility that he would have left some clues behind this time. I hope-"

There was a knock on the door.

"Come in," I replied.

An officer came in.

"Good afternoon ma‘am"

"Afternoon," I nodded, "Straight to the point, please"

"Sure, ma'am. You asked for me to check the CCTV footage of the house of Henry Spark"

"Did you find anything?" Frank asked.

The officer looked at him from head to toe.

"He is with me," I clarified and then, shrugged, "Well, did you?"

"All of the cameras had stopped working just before the crime took place..."

"Typical..." I muttered, bitterness dripping from my words.

"Except..."

The tinge of hope returned and I could feel adrenaline rushing through my body.

"...The back camera. It hasn't captured the criminal's face but it has captured the numberplate of the car in which the criminal made his escape"

I got up hastily, "Circulate the car's number in all police stations. Tell them to catch the owner and that the owner is a wanted criminal. Provide the police with my phone number as well and instruct them to call me directly if they capture the owner or find the car. Tell them not to believe the owner as well. Previously, he got away by showing a fake CIA ID"

"Really?" Frank asked in awe.

"Things get messy and out of hand whenever Soovin Cooper is involved. Officer, it's our biggest lead yet. We might be able to catch Soovin Cooper. Circulate the instructions among all police stations. Put them on high alert"

"Consider it done, ma'am," He saluted and left to put the instructions out.

"Come on Frank, we need to go," I said taking my gun.

"Where?" He said getting up.

"To investigate the crime scene, duh!"

His eyes radiated excitement that made me smile. Then, he obediently followed me out of the headquarters like a child going to a toy shop.

CHAPTER FOUR

# The Unnecessary Spice

The journey by car was progressing smoothly and without any complications. The vehicle was operating efficiently, and we were able to maintain a steady pace on the road. No obstructions or hindrances were impeding our progress, and we were able to enjoy a comfortable and stress-free ride. I and Frank would make occasional small talk to not make the ride boring. However, it turns out that fate had already taken up the job to spice things up for us.

Halfway through the ride, we came across a police check post. After hours of waiting, our turn came and that's when all hell broke loose.

As soon as they saw us, the policeman's face turned grim. He said something on his P25 radio without moving his eyes from us. He swiftly took out his gun and the rest of the officers followed his lead. They all surrounded our car and screamed at us to get out of the car immediately at gunpoint through a megaphone.

"STEP OUT OF THE CAR IMMEDIATELY OR WE WON'T HESITATE TO SHOOT" The voice boomed in my ears.

"WHAT ON EARTH IS GOING ON?!" Frank shouted.

"I DON'T KNOW!" I shouted in reply.

"WE WILL COUNT TILL THREE. IF YOU DON'T COME OUT TILL THEN, WE WILL START FIRING"

"WHAT SHALL WE DO?!" Frank said frantically.

"TRY NOT TO GET SHOT, OF COURSE!" I said while recoiling my seatbelt.

"ONE..."

"HURRY UP, FRANK, YOU WILL GET US KILLED!?" I screamed at Frank who fumbled with his seatbelt.

"TWO..."

I took a deep breath to compose myself and got out before the officer could say three. Frank was at my heel.

They approached us cautiously as if we were some wild animals and they were our zookeepers. When they were near us, they swiftly handcuffed us without opening their mouths.

I cleared my head of all thoughts that would create panic and blur my senses so that I could handle the situation.

"Officer, what is going on?" I asked with confidence that surprised even me.

"Like you don't know, Hannah Gorgin. Who is he?" He pointed the gun toward Frank.

"NO ONE!" Frank said, caught in a frenzy of fear.

"He is my brother and you don't have the right to point your service gun at anyone, officer. That's against the rules" I said sternly.

I had to take control of the situation before the situation overpowered me.

"Is it? A wanted criminal doesn't need to tell *me* about the rules," The policeman scoffed.

"A wanted criminal? There has been a misunderstanding officer. I work for the CIA, for the country!" I exclaimed.

To my surprise, the officer laughed.

"I can show you my batch as well. It's in my pocket" I said, trying to prove my identity while resisting the urge to smack that grin off his face.

"Do you listen that?" he said to his fellow officer, "They said not to believe if he or she shows a fake CIA ID. That trick isn't going to work on us, Miss. Besides, the CIA itself gave us the orders to catch you. So, try something new"

"Wait..."

I and Frank exchanged a look. A horrible suspicion surfaced in my mind

"Under what charge are you arresting us, officer?" I demanded.

"Oh, drop the act, will you?"

"According to the law, even if I am a criminal, I have the right to know on what grounds are you arresting me, AND if you decline that, you are disregarding the rights granted to me by the constitution of the country which is a deed that can get you fired even if you somehow manage to prove me a criminal. So, if you want to keep your job safe, UNDER WHAT CHARGE ARE YOU ARRESTING US?!" I thundered, showing him who the boss was.

The officer gulped. He didn't expect such an outburst but he quickly gathered himself and said, "There are a couple hundred charges against you, according to the CIA. Want me to tell you the most recent one?"

"Spit it out" I glared at him. He was about to push me off my edge and face my wrath once I got out of the mess I was in.

"Killing Henry Spark," He replied through gritted teeth.

I was stunned. They had to catch Soovin, why were they after me? What had caused this power shift and what were the reasons behind it?

"I am the one investigating-"

The policeman cut me off by stuffing a cloth into my mouth and tying it tightly, "That's enough talking. The CIA would question you further. Now, get in the jeep or I will have to use force"

I sighed helplessly. I knew this moron of a policeman won't understand anything even if I told him the truth. So, I went into the jeep in hopes of being interrogated by the CIA officer handling the case - me.

Soon, I was sitting opposite a higher officer. He had white hair, black eyes, and a wrinkled face, indicating that he was fairly experienced.

"Finally caught you," he said smiling, "Now, let's call the officer who is going to extract the confession out of you"

He dialed my number in front of me. It took enormous self-control not to roll my eyes at their boneheadedness.

As soon as he called, my phone kept in my pocket, rang.

He frowned as his confidence started wavering and was gradually replaced with uncertainty. At this point, I wanted to kick some sense into him.

"Um, Rob, remove the cloth from her mouth and put her phone on speaker" He instructed an officer.

The officer who had arrested me freed my mouth, took out my phone, and enabled the speaker.

The senior officer's eyes went wide as the CIA officer he was trying to reach picked up the phone at the exact same moment.

"Police department, here..."

Fear choked him and drowned half his words when his own voice boomed through my phone.

My cold stare said the rest.

"Officer Hannah Gorgin speaking..." I said into my phone just to spite the old man.

I saw all the color drain out of him as his little brain tried to process the change of events.

"Untie both of them, you idiots!" He barked orders at the dumbfounded officers.

I rubbed my wrists where the handcuff had left a mark while maintaining eye contact with the bald officer and continuously giving him a death glare.

Looks like half of this case's frustration was about to be bombarded over these unlucky police officers who were too petrified to speak anything.

Boy, had they made a grave mistake...

CHAPTER FIVE

# Investigation Takes A Turn

Finally, after an entire hour, I and Frank had run out of curses and insulting phrases for the police officers. The poor men could do nothing but listen with their heads down as we gave them a mouthful.

After a while, I decided to calm myself and focus on the case.

"Why did you arrest us?" I asked.

Seeing another opportunity to apologize, the police officer jumped into yet another elaborate explanation, "Ma‘am we are so sorry. It was a misunderstanding-"

"I am asking about that very misunderstanding, officer. Look, we are done whooping you guys-"

"We are?" Frank asked.

I ignored him and continued, "We are redirecting our focus to the case because that’s more important, right Frank?"

Frank nodded half-heartedly. It was visible on his face that he wasn’t done whooping them but I had to be the guide, pointing out our actual priorities, as usual.

"So, officer, tell me how you came to the conclusion that I was the wanted criminal-"

"Even when you had just one job that you messed up horribly-" Frank interrupted in between, clearly wanting to go back to whooping.

I ignored him as usual, "-And if you miss even a single detail...well, you have just gotten a demo. Things might get physical as well, so..."

The officer, Rob, wiped the sweat off his forehead and began spilling the tea, "Ma'am, we were provided with both your contact number and your vehicle's registration number. Upon conducting a thorough investigation, we were able to successfully trace the registration number of the vehicle in question, which ultimately led us to discover your name"

I frowned at first and then, scowled as the realization hit me. Soovin Cooper doesn't make mistakes. He left-

"Instead of solving the case in your mind, would you care to tell me as well?" Frank groaned impatiently after reading my facial expressions.

I said, "Soovin Cooper left the back camera working, it wasn't a mistake. He wanted us to see it. That jerk used my car to escape so that the police would come after me. This was a diversion so-"

"So that he can get enough time to go underground," Frank completed, "This guy really is a genius...No offense to you, of course," He quickly added after seeing my expression.

I sighed. The room was silent for a moment. Everyone was lost in his own sea of thoughts. Mine revolved around how badly I wanted to strangle that lunatic.

Finally, I broke the silence, "We should go to the crime scene as soon as possible. I don't fancy the idea of us going

to investigate in the dark"

"Okay but...Why?" Frank asked with a frown.

"Because it is not safe, genius. Soovin might be hanging around the corner in case he forgot to take care of an important clue and that guy wouldn't mind killing two people on his way"

Frank gulped, "Not sure how I feel about that..."

"But it will probably be fine. I will send a team to Henry's house to arrange everything till we reach. Gathering clues and calling Henry's family for interrogation and all, you know?"

"I don't know but hell, I am ready for investigating!" Frank exclaimed.

His childish enthusiasm brought a smile to my face despite the circumstances. It was then, I realized maybe this unusual duo of a CIA officer and her engineer brother wasn't entirely pathetic. He knew when and how to lighten the mood and keep the spirits up while I had the expertise needed to solve the case.

The police officers apologized one last time for the horrible misunderstanding before I and Frank continued our journey to the crime scene.

Soon, we were standing outside Henry's home with a loyal armed team in case things were to get messy. His family had been called for investigation as well. Now, I was pretty confident that they weren't the mastermind behind Henry's demise but they might lead us to the actual killer by helping us and I could bet that it was Soovin Cooper.

I glanced at each one of them, studying their faces for a touch of either fear or guilt. I frowned as something bugged me in the back of my mind. Something or rather *someone* was missing.

Henry's brother was staring at the horizon with hollow eyes. His wife was blinking back tears. Henry's mother was about to faint from all crying and no food while his father was trying to hold her, swallowing his own tears.

But...Where was his daughter?

"Where is Henry Spark's daughter?" I asked the family.

Henry's brother looked up as if the spell gluing his eyes to the horizon had finally been broken.

"She is staying at my house," he replied.

"Where is she at the moment?" I asked.

"She was at my house, the last time I checked" He replied dreamily.

I sighed and continued, though not letting go of the girl's absence, "Who lives with you at your house?"

"Me, my wife, and my parents...Now, Anna too"

"So, Soovin lived alone with his daughter in this house?"

"Mom and Dad alternate between our houses every month. So, for the time being, yes, only he, and Anna were there"

"So, you have a caretaker of some kind at your home or...?"

"No, we divide the work"

"Wait, so, Anna is currently alone in that house of yours?" I asked with wide eyes.

"She...wouldn't come. She hasn't spoken a word since Henry..." He wiped a stray tear from his dry cheeks.

"Do you have any amiable neighbors?"

"No, our house is kind of apart. We like privacy. Will you stop asking questions about my house. This is supposed to be about Henry-"

"So, you left a six-year-old girl on her own with nobody to help her in case of emergency, right after her dad was MURDERED BY SOMEONE?!" I screamed at the moron of an uncle facing me.

His eyes widened as it dawned on him.

"DO YOU EVEN HAVE A BRAIN?!" Frank screamed as the realization hit him like a thunderstorm.

I decided to act fast as a moment might cost Anna's life, "Frank, start the car. One of you get inside the car. We need guidance to get to the house. OFFICERS! Escot this vehicle to its destination. A six-year-old girl's life is at stake! Come on, hurry!"

Frank swiftly started the engine as I and Henry's brother dashed into the car. Now, it was a race against time and luck with a six-year-old girl's life being the trophy dangling in between.

CHAPTER SIX

# Soovin And Hannah's Face-Off

Two police cars in front and two at back, with their sirens wailing, both of them guarding a black Scorpio which is going at the speed of an airplane is quite a sight. However, all I could think about at that time was Anna. The face of the poor girl resurfaced and submerged in my mind a billion times. I could see her at the mercy of Soovin in my mind. The thought made my blood boil.

I promised myself that I wouldn't let anything happen to that girl. From now on, she was my responsibility. Soovin wouldn't lay a finger on her.

I hoped against all odds that we were just overreacting and the girl was playing at her uncle's home but deep down, I somehow knew that wasn't the case. My sixth sense which had developed a lot in my seven years of service was on high alert. It was warning me that this wasn't right and the girl was in grave danger. It had caused an adrenaline rush whose effects didn't seem to vanish anytime soon.

I felt hopeless. The most I could do was scream at Frank to drive faster even when he was driving at a speed that would have given Mom a heart attack. I felt glad that he understood my mindset and how I was overwhelmed with worries. Being the amazing brother he was, he didn't bite back. That guy knew me inside out.

A wave of discomfort washed over me, settling deep in the pit of my stomach and causing a sinking sensation that weighed heavily on my mind. As much as I tried to shake it off, I couldn't believe that the girl was safe and sound.

After what felt like a year of guilt, frustration, and anticipation building up inside my chest to burst out like a volcano at any given time, we finally reached their home.

I dashed out and violently closed the car door with a snap. My eyes darted towards the door of the house. It was wide open. I was right. Soovin was here.

I took out my gun with confidence. Hesitation seemed to be a foreign concept. I was ready to penetrate Soovin's skull with a round of bullets.

I turned to my brother, "Frank, things have gotten serious. You will stay here with these officers-"

"While you go out and check the house? HELL, NO! I AM COMING!" Frank thundered.

I turned to the officers, "Hold him down if necessary but keep him right here, in your sight. There should not be even a single scratch on my brother. His safety is your responsibility. Tie him down if needed but protect him with all you have got"

"No worries ma'am. No one will lay even a finger on your brother, " The officers assured me.

Frank interrupted once again, under the misunderstanding that I was in the mood to give an ear to him, "Han, it-"

"SHUT UP AND LET ME DO MY DUTY, FRANK!?" I screamed at the top of my lungs while running towards the building.

I checked my gun. It was loaded and Soovin's name was written on every single bullet. I wouldn't let him touch the girl.

I gathered my thoughts and cleared my head while leaning against the door and looking at the bright stars in the dark night.

My only aim? Protect Anna at any cost and if anyone dares to come in between, show him no mercy, shoot without any hesitation.

With all my priorities sorted in under ten seconds, I tiptoed into the house, light and quick on my feet, ready to pounce at a second's notice.

The house was eerily quiet, like the calm before the storm. I made my way towards the light switch. I tried the lights but the electricity had been cut off.

*Typical,* I thought bitterly.

I glanced around. All the doors were open as if someone had been searching every room for something or *someone.* There were somehow no signs of violence yet which was a good sign for my anger and Soovin's life.

I froze as I heard footsteps. First heavy and confident ones followed by tiny, light, and faint ones.

*Soovin and Anna*, my mind supplied.

I rushed towards the sound, my patience long gone, buried under layers of emotions. As my pace quickened, so did the footsteps. I somehow heard the sound of a window breaking over my heart pounding in my ears loud enough to deafen me.

I increased my pace. I turned around the final corner, fully aware that the source of the sound was behind it.

I caught a mere glimpse of a six-foot-tall, masculine figure holding a little girl before the man threw some broken glass shards at me. I covered my face with my hand to deflect the shards from causing any serious damage. I felt them smash into my covered arm and cut the clothing in several places.

When I looked back after recovering from the surprise attack, I saw the back of the man jumping through the window swiftly.

I pounced at the window but only managed to graze the man's shirt before he glided down. I regained my balance and peered down from the window. There he was.

My eyes met his green orbs. His angular jaw was suited with a fair complexion. His black hair was silky smooth. His lips were as red as a pomegranate. Upon seeing me, they curved up into a smile or rather a smirk of triumph. His eyes shined with a spark of accomplishment. He looked up, grinning like the devil he was.

He tightened his arms around the girl who was on his back. Judging from her lack of movement, she was probably asleep or unconscious. Knowing Soovin, the latter was much more possible.

"I will get you one day, Soovin," I said in a firm tone.

"I would like to see you try, darling" He replied in a calm tone as if we were old pals meeting after a long time.

Then, his smirk disappeared, "Stay away," He looked hither and tither with indecisiveness and a hint of nervousness, which I had witnessed the first time on his overconfident face.

"Look, Hannah, I am trying to-"

Suddenly, the cops fired in his direction.

Soovin's first instinct was to cover the girl.

"DON'T SHOOT! HE HAS THE GIRL WITH HIM!" I hollered.

The firing stopped as Soovin made a run for it but not before screaming, "Thanks, sweetheart!" just to spite me.

I kicked the wall near me in an effort to release my anger and frustration but it was in vain because the emotions kept on building at an alarming rate.

He had taken Anna...and escaped successfully right under my nose. He had outsmarted me again. I promised myself that it would be the last time and I would get him back for it. I would retrieve Anna from him and drag him to the court myself.

CHAPTER SEVEN

# Breaking Leads To Building

I stormed out of the house with flames of rage eating my heart out, the guilt was crushing my spirits as well. My first command should have been to surround the building with officers. Instead, selfish me had posted them for Frank's security. I should have thought this through before storming into the building. It was all my fault and now, I had to tell Henry's family that I couldn't save Henry's daughter either.

The moment I stepped out of the house, Henry's brother and Frank scurried toward me.

"What happened?" They asked together.

After a moment of silence, I finally replied, "They are gone...Both Soovin and Anna"

Henry's brother grabbed his hair and screamed in frustration and anger. On the other hand, Frank watched me with concern.

He whispered in my ear in a tender voice, "You good, Han?"

I nodded while blinking back tears.

Frank didn't seem convinced. He said, "It's night already, let's get home"

I nodded once more, too caught up in my own thoughts and drained by my mind to reply verbally. Besides, I knew that if I said anything, my voice would crack and I would break down bewailing.

I approached the team of officers, fully aware of how hard it would be for me to break the news to them. All our efforts to get here had gone down the drain.

Gathering all my courage and energy, I said, "We lost them...Soovin has escaped with Anna..."

"We apologize ma'am. It's our fault, we should have surrounded the building-" One of the officers said.

"All you are responsible for is to follow my orders. I am the one who failed to give the most basic order. I failed to see past my selfish goal to protect my brother. None of you is to blame except me...I am sorry for this, officers"

"Ma'am, it's not your-" Another officer tried to speak.

"Good night, officers. You can go and rest. I will call you guys up tomorrow if I require assistance in this case"

They sighed and gave me a half-hearted salute, their faces portrayed disappointment which made me want to curl up in a ball and cry my eyes out.

"Come on, Han. Let's go home" Frank said as gently as possible which just made it harder to swallow my tears.

We both got into the car and settled in our seats. Frank started the engine as we embarked on our journey back.

Frank's eyes diverted from the road to me and then to the road repeatedly while I stared out of the window at the dark sky. Soon, it started raining. It seemed as if the sky was weeping for me, letting go of the tears I couldn't. The tears I wouldn't allow to surface and was swallowing then and again, the tears which were now accumulating as grief inside me.

I was drowning in guilt. My own emotions were choking me. I couldn't stand it. I had failed once again that too to the same criminal.

"Han, we are home," Frank whispered gently, breaking my vicious train of thoughts that was about to run over my confidence and dignity as an officer.

I got out dreamily, too preoccupied with myself, trying my best to hold on to something, frantically and desperately trying to find a positive aspect to keep me from flowing with the negativity into an endless dark pit. I entered the house, barely aware of anything happening around me. All I could focus on was fighting this inner battle.

"Can you order something, Frank? I am not in a position to make something right now," I asked Frank airily.

"Sure, how does burger and fries sound?" he asked with an excited smile, trying to cheer me up.

"Great," I replied nonchalantly, "I will just take a quick shower till the food arrives"

I went to my room with heavy steps.

I entered the shower to gather my thoughts but it was proving to be a rather hard task. My mind was a mess of thoughts and I was having a hard time trying not to get pulverized beneath them. I felt the weight of a mountain upon my chest.

When I was finally alone in the shower, I allowed myself to come undone. The running water muffled my cries as I helplessly tried to overcome my emotions. I pounded my fists on the wall while weeping.

"Han, the food has arrived!" I heard Frank shout.

I jerked back. I wiped my tears helplessly and replied in a firm voice that surprised even me, "Coming, Frank!"

Finally, I gathered myself and came outside the bathroom, having changed from my formal uniform to comfortable clothing. My eyes lingered on the CIA badge I had left on my bed before the shower.

Although I knew I shouldn't, I began questioning myself, *Do I really deserve this?*

I brushed the thoughts away once more and went to the dining room where Frank was waiting for me with food.

We ate in silence for a while.

Then, Frank spoke, "You know, it really wasn't your fault"

His words echoed off the walls.

I suddenly became very interested in my burger.

"Han, you have arrested hundreds of criminals failing to catch one doesn't mean you failed..."

"What else does it mean, Frank?" I asked with bloodshot eyes.

"It means that you have got another chance to catch him in a better way with solid proof. You might catch him red-handed next time. Look at the positive side!"

Frank's efforts to cheer me up brought a smile to my face as always.

"I am sorry, Han. If I hadn't forced you to make me a part of this, maybe you would have caught-"

"I am just happy that you got to experience this and live your dream for a while, Frank. Now, you are stuck with me on this case and you are not leaving in between because I won't be able to solve this case without you, can I?"

We both laughed at that. It was genuine laughter, not the forced one I use to hide my emotions. The tension between us melted away and was replaced with the warmth of sibling love. We happily finished the rest of our meal while laughing and joking around with each other.

My thoughts of failure were long forgotten and were pushed to the back of my mind. We were having a good time until my phone rang.

The hair on my neck stood up for no apparent reason and then, I looked at the screen flashing *'Private Number'*. It's times like these when I curse my sixth sense and my retentivity.

I had a minor flashback and somehow, I knew it was him. Soovin had always enjoyed mocking me after making an escape but at the moment, thanks to the change in my attitude and thinking Frank had caused, I saw this as my chance to get my hands on a clue.

CHAPTER EIGHT

# AN AMUSING CALL

I picked the phone up and cleared my head. I had to focus on every single detail. I turned on the recording to review the call in the future. Every insignificant detail needed to be analyzed when it came to Soovin Cooper.

"Hello, Soovin," I said coldly.

Frank listened to the conversation with rapt attention on hearing Soovin's name.

"Hey there, sweetheart!" He said in his usual overconfident manner.

"What do you need?" I had to pretend to be irritated and eager to cut the call so that he wouldn't get suspicious, lower his guard, and leave some clues behind.

"I just wanted to check on you, you know? Make sure you are not beating yourself up because of me"

"You don't need to take my care. Embrace *yourself*, Soovin, I will get you soon"

"That same old dialogue, ha?" Soovin said casually with a hint of admiration in his voice, "Haven't you gotten tired of this rivalry between us? Stop chasing me, girl. I have had enough and I know that you have had too"

I heard the sound of a train but it wasn't accompanied by any rustling of wind.

"Stop playing games, Soovin. I am a CIA officer for goodness's sake! I can differentiate between a recorded train sound and a real one. Drop the act, will you?" I said as a smirk crept upon my lips.

Soovin laughed merrily and said, "Can't blame me for trying, can you? Just checking if you were rusty or not. Oh god, Han, I have realized that you haven't tried to track my number this time"

"As if you haven't already made sure that I can't track your number, you brainiac"

"Glad you finally dropped the idea. It was getting a bit mundane if I be honest"

"Now, stop playing games and come to the point, will you? You might be free or not in the mood to plan your next act but I don't have time for this"

He sighed, "Fine. I want to bring this thing to an end"

"Which *thing?*" I frowned.

"You following me everywhere, watching my every goddamn move and all. Look, we had an encounter and I won fair and square. Now, let's just forget about each other and stop interfering in the other's work. Let each other live their own life, and do their own job. You mind your own businesses and I will mind mine"

"My job *is* to catch you, genius"

"I knew you wouldn't let me go so easily. Someone has got a fancy for me, I suppose?" I could almost hear him smile.

Suddenly, a little girl's muffled and faint voice came. However, it wasn't urgent or fearful but calm and at peace.

"Anna is with you?" I asked, genuinely concerned for the little girl.

"You were there when I...you know?"

"Kidnapped her?" I supplied with a hint of anger.

"What? No! I have just...taken her. Kidnapped sounds a bit absurd here, doesn't it? Now, I will come to the real point. You don't need to worry about Anna. She will be safe with me"

"What makes you believe I am worrying about my case's...victim's daughter? She isn't even a witness" I put a hard edge to my voice. If he got to know that I was concerned about the girl, he might use it against me.

"Come on, Han! This isn't the first time we have crossed paths. We have dealt with each other quite a few times, now. And as much as you would hate to admit it, we know each other almost like best friends at this point"

"CIA and a wanted assassin can never be friends"

"I am not a *wanted assassin*, okay!?" I heard pure frustration and a touch of disgust in his voice but he quickly masked his emotions, "I just do a job...like you do"

I decided to drop the topic, "Why are you telling me this? And How can I believe that a..." I caught myself, recalling his anger, "...criminal like you would keep Anna safe?"

"I am telling *you* this, Officer Hannah Gorgin because you aren't like other officers," It took a moment for me to realize that he was actually serious, "You don't treat people as stone-hearted beings who are nothing but mere suspects or victims. You actually feel human emotions, unlike half of your *CIA,"* The way he said *CIA* radiated pure hatred and repugnance.

"What do you mean?"

"Don't act innocent. Even you know that the CIA no longer serves the people. It just protects a sheet made by people years ago with baseless-"

"Are you referring to our constitution?" I asked in disbelief.

"Yes, I am, " He said without hesitation, "It's about time that document got up to date"

"I see no way that *that* justifies you killing innocent people!"

"It doesn't but...Let's not get into my personal life, officer. I just want you to stop worrying about Anna and drop this case. If you do that...You won't be hearing from me anymore"

"Are you implying that you are going straight?" I asked in disbelief.

"Yes"

The seriousness in his voice made me laugh out loud.

"Are you the same Soovin Cooper I know?" I said in between laughter, "You are out of your mind if you think that you can get away from all this by pretending that you suddenly woke up and realized that you should change that too over a *phone call* like a coward"

"Now, what does *that* mean?" He said fiercely.

"It means that if you really wanted to change, you would have come to me like a man, looked me dead in the eye, and told me you wanted to change. Then, maybe surrendered and started a new life!"

"I don't have time to spend in jail," He replied in a clear-cut tone.

"Really? *That's* your reason?"

"I am a busy man with a tight schedule, woman. I can't wait to turn over a new leaf. I am short on time and patience"

"Great excuse to chicken out, Soovin. I am kind of disappointed in you now. I thought you were a daredevil"

"I *am* a daredevil, girl"

"I don't know about daredevil but you are a coward for sure"

He remained silent for a while. It was long enough that I had to confirm that the line wasn't dead.

Then, he said in a grim voice that gave me goosebumps, "Turn around"

CHAPTER NINE

# DUTY OR EMOTIONS...?

My heart almost stopped. My brain was bubbling with anticipation. Could he somehow be here...?

There was only one way to find out. I turned around as my heart pounded in my ears, loud enough to make me flinch.

My wandering glance fixated at one point. My eyes stopped dead in their tracks when they came across a pair of green eyes staring right into my soul.

Soovin was standing on the roof of our neighbor.

Frank gulped loudly as he saw Soovin as well. He put a hand on my shoulder while his eyes were glued to Soovin. Frank was too shocked to do anything else and so was I. So, we both just stared at him for a solid minute.

But Soovin's eyes were staring at me and only me. He wasn't blinking. I wanted to break our eye contact for it was making my heartbeat skyrocket but I couldn't. I felt like those green eyes were capturing mine. I was unable to blink even when my eyes started watering a bit.

Then, he looked me dead in the eye, and screamed, "I WANT TO CHANGE!?"

I flinched on hearing the scream and blinked instinctively. I finally came to my senses as if the spell he was casting on me had broken. I reached for my gun hastily and aimed at him.

It was a clear and easy shot. I could have killed him right there and then but I hesitated to pull the trigger. The practical and professional side of my brain was screaming at me to pull the trigger and close Soovin's hundred or so files. This was my best shot at catching him, no, killing him. On the other hand, the other part of my brain didn't allow me to pull the trigger. It was drowning in sentiments and emotions. Our conversation over the phone was replaying in my head. I was torn apart between my duty and emotions.

I was fighting myself, neglecting my duty for *him, Soovin Cooper.* I had never thought that such a day would come but here I was, hand on the trigger, gun aimed straight at him but still, unable to pull the trigger.

His green eyes were begging me for trust. A part of me wanted to believe in him and give him another chance at life but the other part of me wondered if this was just an act for another one of his devious plots.

Soovin didn't show even a glimpse of surprise when I didn't pull the trigger as if he knew what was going on in my mind...as if he knew the *inner me.*

He raised his hand with the phone. I understood him and picked up my phone which had fallen down in the midst of this chaos.

"This very hesitation makes you different from other robots working in the CIA, Hannah...This is the thing I admire about you...This is why...I am asking you for help," His voice cracked in the end as if he was fighting tears.

I paid more attention to his face to judge his sincerity. His green eyes were now misty. Even the ghost of his signature smirk wasn't there. He was emotional and serious instead of overconfident and easy-going as usual.

Before I could process anything more, which I doubted I could even in a year, the neighbors saw Soovin and screamed loud enough to wake the entire town.

Just like that, within a blink of an eye, he was gone. Vanished into thin air. Made his escape like the prodigy he was.

"Hannah?" Frank's voice broke whatever stance I was in.

"Oh god..." I muttered with my head in my hands.

"I underestimated you. Your job sure can be dangerous..." Frank said.

I was trying my best not to overburden my brain with thoughts revolving around Soovin. This little incident had impacted me a lot more than it should have. He could have shot at us quietly from up there, whatever way he reached there. I realized the security of my home was disturbingly low and as weak as a lamb that can't stand the weight of its own wool.

"Just when I think things can't get any more complicated, life gets offended and takes it as a challenge. It's been a hell of a day..." I groaned into my hand.

Frank laughed, easing the tension, and said, "Even for a CIA officer like you?"

"Even for a CIA officer like me," I affirmed.

"So...What are you going to do? Will you help him or...?"

"Firstly, I will make sure that you don't eavesdrop on any more calls of mine"

"Come on! Don't change the topic, Han. What are you thinking?"

I sighed heavily, "I can't even process what I am thinking right now. My mind is a mess of thoughts, Frank. I am...overwhelmed with...every goddamn thing"

"Maybe because it's well past your bedtime"

I looked at my wristwatch which read '12:01 AM'.

"I have to get up at six in the morning for investigation. God, I need to get some rest! I am going to faint from exhaustion..." I said moving toward my bedroom.

Frank followed me, "Are you telling me that you will be able to sleep when all hell has broken loose in this case...?"

I replied, "Yes, that's exactly what I am saying. Don't underestimate the power of exhaustion, Frank. Whatever happens, things can't possibly get any more complex...I mean even if they do, I will handle them tomorrow with a fresh mind. A tired mind will just overcomplicate the problems if it's possible. It won't do me any good but ruin everything"

I entered my bedroom and turned to face Frank who was standing at the door, shaking his head.

"Damn...Your job is full of stress and tension. I am kind of glad I didn't pass the exam and made my life a horror movie"

I smiled and then, fighting the sleepiness in my eyelids, I said, "Remember, Frank, with a great deal of stress comes an even more important need to rest and clear your head. Wake me at 5:30 AM sharp, please, buddy!"

With that, I closed the door. I breathed in the familiar cologne of my room that calmed my racing mind and eased the frown on my forehead.

I suddenly grew aware of how much my body was screaming with pain due to my habit of continuously challenging and crossing my body's limits. I really needed to focus on my health along with work or I won't end up in a good condition.

Then, I wasted no more time and literally collapsed on the bed like a dead man. I allowed the exhaustion to take over me entirely as I gradually drifted into sleep when my entire life was caught in a thunderstorm named - 'Soovin Cooper'.

CHAPTER TEN

# Overcoming Dead Ends

I slowly opened my eyelids and allowed the light to activate my brain. I checked the time, it was 5 AM. I got up and stretched my muscles, ready to get the day started.

Then, I plugged in my earphones and did some workout while my mind revolved around the one and only - Soovin Cooper.

I was desperately trying to find a solution to this Soovin problem but I was having no luck at it. I replayed our conversation three times in an effort to gather my thoughts which were overflooding beyond my control.

My heart said that for once, Soovin was telling the truth. He actually wanted to turn over a new leaf but my mind warned me about his cleverness and wickedness. His mind was as complicated as it gets. It was an endless labyrinth of plots and schemes, none of them in accordance with the law, values, or correct principles.

After fighting an inner battle, I came to the conclusion that I needed to know what caused his humanity to suddenly wake up if anything like that happened at all. And if he really wanted to go straight, then who was I to stop him and push him into the pit of the illegal world again? If he had really started to regret his past, then, he deserved a chance.

But, I needed information to find that. I had realized my mistake. I was searching Henry's family and his home, just what Soovin had expected, and probably didn't leave any more clues behind that way. He knew me, that was the problem. He knew who I was going to investigate and where I would look for clues, so, he made sure to erase his trace from that path. I had to follow the same method as him. I needed to know who I was dealing with. I needed to understand him inside out to speculate whether this was sincere or just an act.

However, I couldn't close Henry's case by stating that the murderer wants to change. So, the question still lingered in my mind, *Shouldn't he be punished for taking an innocent life and destroying a happy and harmless family?*

After scanning my conscience for answers, I realized it all came down to one question, Was Soovin guilty or not...? And to answer that, I needed to know why he killed Henry Spark. Heck, he came out of his bill premature to take this man down! He wouldn't risk his life for a simple contract. Even an important and expensive contract didn't justify his concealed anger imprinted on Henry's very body. This was something else...something personal.

I needed to dig into Henry's and Soovin's life, past and present. Every minute detail was important. There *had* to be a connection between them, official or unofficial.

"Woah! You awake?" Frank said groggily rubbing his sleepy eyelids.

"Ya, we need to get to the headquarters, Frank"

"Did something happen?" Frank asked with an almost terrified look.

He sighed in relief as I smiled and replied, "Nothing happened. We need to move on with the investigation. I have promised myself that today would be the last day of this case"

"Someone's feeling confident, today. That's good. Keep the spirits up!"

He smiled at the apparent flames of determination in my eyes. I just had a feeling that I was extremely close to finding out the truth and unveiling the mystery. My sixth sense confirmed that I was on the right track. I just needed to run faster.

During the car ride to the headquarters, I took the opportunity to share all my thoughts and ideas with Frank. I wanted to make sure that he was fully informed and up-to-date on everything that was going on, and I will admit it, I valued his input and perspective. Though we weren't really on the same page, we had a common goal aligned with correct values unlike Soovin - To make sure justice is served, whether it is a criminal or a civilian.

Soon, we both were sitting in my cabin with two cups of coffee. I was engrossed in my laptop, digging up all files of Soovin Cooper and Henry Spark while Frank attacked his grilled cheese sandwich.

I hit the brakes too soon, an hour to be precise. I had reached all dead ends and didn't know where to go next.

I dumped all the important information in one place to help me connect the dots, the place being Frank's dumb yet bright mind.

"It turns out Henry visited this club almost daily and came home often heavily drunk. He indulged in drinking when his wife passed away and soon became addicted to it. He tried leaving it but couldn't"

"That's all fine but...where does Soovin come into the picture?"

"Nowhere. That's the issue. I have checked a billion times but nothing ties them together. I have come to the conclusion that whatever ties them together isn't recorded anywhere, probably an unofficial bond buried inside just Soovin and Henry. Now, that brings us to Soovin Cooper"

Frank straightened in his chair and gestured me to start, "Soovin Cooper himself doesn't know anything about his family. He grew up in a lonely orphanage with no one to rely upon. However, he made one friend there. His name isn't specified but Soovin and him were one soul, two bodies. That's when all started going south. His friend died in a demonstration against the government. The poor teenage boy got trampled upon as the demonstrators rushed to get away from the police. That turned Soovin against the government. It was at that time, that he fell into not bad but horrible and illegal company. He was young and crazy and *someone* decided to take advantage of his hatred"

I caught my breath as Frank said impatiently, "Don't leave me hanging!"

"Have some patience, Frank. Humans like me need to breathe. You wouldn't know. Anyways, by a series of events, he got into the network of illegal dealers. He began helping them to earn a living in order to leave the orphanage which reminded him that the hole in his heart had no replacement. He decided to call his own shots. That's how he entered into the criminal world. From there, he made his way up to become the most wanted assassin in the country"

"Man...Not gonna lie, his story is kind of inspiring"

"He is a *criminal*, Frank!"

"You are accessing the situation as a CIA officer, Han. For a moment, picture the whole story as a little child who doesn't have a sense of wrong or right. According to him, he *was* and *is* doing the right thing. He believes that this is the correct way to go"

"But it isn't!" I exclaimed with wide eyes.

"He thinks otherwise"

"He thinks that killing anyone just for money is correct?" I asked in disbelief.

Frank rolled his eyes at me, thought for a bit, and said, "Do you have a list of all his past victims, targets, or whatever the hell they are called?"

"Ya...? Where are you going with this Frank?"

"Just believe me this once. Read out the list, not the names but their contribution and what they basically stood for or did"

I hit some keys on my laptop, then, read aloud, "Most recent one before Henry is an influential leader, a rich businessman, another assassin, a drug dealer-"

"I was right! He has killed only the people who were *not* innocent. He isn't a villain like the CIA and the entire world portrays him"

"Why do you keep on idolizing him? He is a criminal! Get this fact imprinted in your mind"

"Han, the rivalry you have with him is restricting your view, it's blinding you! Try to look beyond that veil of hatred. He isn't downright evil and wicked. Your mind is conditioning you to think that way. Take the control back"

I tried to think about it but my patience got the best of me, "This is not a movie or a story, Frank! Besides, he did this not for some noble cause but only because their rival gang gave him the contract to kill those people with the promise of money"

Frank shook his head and said, "That's the problem with you CIA officers. You all get so caught up in weighing the pros and cons, causes, and consequences of every situation that you tend to forget to see the bigger picture. Han, look beyond the details. What was the final outcome of his deed despite who he did it for or why he did it?"

I closed my eyes in thought. Processing all Frank's previous and current words. It took some time to convince my mind but in the end, I knew I was wrong. Frank's every single word was correct.

I opened my eyes and said, "That some *not-so-innocent* people died"

"Exactly my point!" Frank said, throwing his head back in his chair like a kid who had just solved a math problem of higher level in class.

CHAPTER ELEVEN

# Soovin Makes A Mistake

"But Frank, there is one problem," I said which made Frank groan.

"Can't shut down the CIA side of my brain, can I?" I said smiling.

"Always pointing out the mistakes...What is it?" Frank said with a mocking smile.

"Henry is the odd one here. He wasn't involved in crimes at all. I have checked his record myself, as clean as a sheet, let me tell you. All he has done is cross the red light once"

"Henry seems to be the odd one from multiple angles, doesn't he?" Frank asked.

I thought and said, "Ya. For starters, he wasn't involved in crimes at all. Judging by the untidy looks of the crime scene, Soovin had acted on impulse. He hadn't done much prior planning which is unlike him. All his previous kills have been so smoothly planned and executed that I would have not believed Soovin had killed Henry if it was not for his handprints and him kidnapping Anna in front of my eyes"

"Maybe that guy isn't actually Soovin but a look-alike...?"

I shook my head in disbelief, my mind refusing what my ears had heard, "I think you should give your pea-sized brain some rest. This case has driven you mad and you are driving *me* mad. Really, Frank? A goddamn look-alike? That's the best guess you can make?"

Suddenly, an officer busted through my door, panting like a dog.

"Officer! Have you ever heard of knocking?!" I screamed.

"Sorry....ma'am, I just..." He said breathlessly.

"Okay, take deep breaths," Frank tried to calm the officer down, "Copy my breathing, buddy"

The officer took several deep breaths and once he had calmed down, he said in a single breath, "Ma'am, Soovin Cooper has been spotted in an amusement park with Anna. He tried to hide his face from the cameras. However, Anna was disguised as well, though rather horribly. We have used her eye scan to identify her as you instructed. The eye scan confirms that it's Anna and she has been spotted with a six-foot-tall man, matching Soovin's profile!"

I and Frank jumped up from our seats. I grabbed my gun and Frank grabbed the car keys.

"Officer, declare high alert. Immediately instruct six parties of cops to surround the building, leaving no space. Not even a fly should be able to leave the amusement park. Send twelve undercover agents to merge with the crowd and keep an evasive eye on Soovin. Make sure they haven't encountered Soovin before so that Soovin gets no chance to comprehend their actual purpose. You yourself keep a watchful eye on every single camera of that park and keep me updated on his every move. We are rushing towards the park right now," I fixed an earpiece on Frank and myself,

"Guide us toward him through the earpiece. Inform our meritorious team of officers who had assisted us yesterday that their service is needed and I have summoned them in urgency. HURRY!"

The officer ran to enforce all the orders while I and Frank made a run for the parking lot.

All the officers assembled near my car.

"This is not a drill, officers!" I quickly gave them the necessary information spiked with a motivating pep-talk.

Four police cars and one black Scorpio rushed out of the headquarters. Even on the streets, our soaring speed won many quizzical looks from on-lookers but none of us gave them a single thought.

All of us had one clear aim in mind which was bounding us together - Arrest Soovin and secure Anna at all costs. Well, maybe the aim wasn't shared by one of us.

"Are you going to arrest him?" Frank asked with a hint of worry.

"Yes," I replied without hesitation.

"Hannah, the people he killed were-"

"What about Henry, Frank? Even if he killed just one innocent man, supposing that the others were criminals, still, he has taken an innocent man's life and that can't be overlooked. It's our duty to protect the nation from such-"

"Maybe Henry wasn't innocent and we are missing something!"

"Stop defending him!" I took a deep breath to calm myself, "We will extract the truth out of him in the interrogation room"

"And then what...?"

"The court will decide it, Frank. I don't have that power"

"But-"

"Enough! Firstly, we need to arrest him. Focus on the present, Frank!"

I jumped out of the car the second it slowed down near the entry of the park. It was quite a sight to see.

The amusement park was surrounded by innumerable officers who were fully alert and had their guns ready to shoot at my mere command. Two officers were explaining the situation to the park authorities and instructing them to not create a panic and give the most wanted assassin the benefit of chaos and an opportunity to flee.

"Ma'am," I heard a familiar voice in my earpiece, "Am I audible? Over"

"Crystal clear, officer. Great and efficient work at your end. Remind me to inform Boss that someone deserves a promotion. Over"

"It's my pleasure, ma'am. Over"

"Where is he at the moment? Over" I asked.

"He is at the water fountain at the center of the park, in a clown outfit with Anna who is in a lion suit. Over"

I turned towards Frank, "Come on, Frank! Let's complete Soovin's file once and for all"

I only saw uncertainty dancing on his face.

"He is a *criminal,* Frank. No matter how hard you try to deny it, his path was wrong and that's a fact. I understand that he didn't know what was right and what was wrong but he still made the wrong choice even if he thinks otherwise"

I could tell that Frank wanted to argue but he didn't and we entered the park.

We made our way through hundreds of innocent families who were unaware of the fact that a wanted criminal was roaming among them.

Finally, I reached the center of the park and saw a clown and a little girl in a lion's suit sitting near the fountain.

"He is playing with her and filling her life with happiness, Han..."

I turned towards him to confront him and clear his doubts once and for all, "I can't assure you his punishment, Frank, but I can assure you that I will give him a fair chance, ignoring our rocky past and heated rivalry. If I somehow find him not guilty of any crime, I will not let him get punished. You *know* that I don't give a damn about the rules of the CIA. I am a lady of principles. If he doesn't deserve to be punished, I will find a way out for him. I will make sure justice is served to *everyone.* I will keep the promise we made"

Frank smiled, "I trust you"

I finally saw his face cleared of uncertainty. Now, he was no longer my weakness but my strength. Now, I was sure I could count on him and he would have my back if things were to go down in any way.

I glanced around us. It took my experienced eyes mere seconds to locate the undercover agents camouflaging among the crowd.

"Officer, connect the undercover agents with me. Over"

After a moment, my earpiece buzzed, "Ma'am they are all connected now. Over"

I took charge, "Officers, that clown is our target. He is an ace at martial arts and can kill us with a snap of his finger if we are not attentive. Slowly approach them...Form a circle around me and him..."

I wasn't going to make the same mistake. Learning from mistakes transforms them from a failure to a step towards success.

I continued, "Now, the officer in the white shirt and I will approach the target gradually while you all be ready and strengthen the circle. Officers, make sure that the girl isn't harmed. There shouldn't be a single scratch on her. Frank, for your own protection, you will stay close to me. As close as my shadow, got it?"

"Shadow in mid-day...? Sure"

I rolled my eyes at him and continued, "At my count of three, all of you will take out your guns, aimed at the target. I will hold his hands behind his back while the other officer who I have instructed to approach the target with me will pick up the girl and secure her in his arms. This all should happen together, in a fraction of a second. Are you guys ready?"

Multiple voices reached my ears all filled with determination and speaking the same phrase - "Yes, ma'am!"

"One"

I watched all of their hands go inside their jacket as I myself felt for my gun. I gripped its handle so tight that my knuckles whitened. My heart was beating a million times a second.

"Two"

We all loaded our guns. Adrenaline surged through my body. Years of chase were about to end. This. Was. It.

"THREE!" I screamed at the top of my lungs as chaos unfurled.

CHAPTER TWELVE

# A Magical Connection

With a swift motion, I had Soovin's hands held behind his back while the officer scooped up Anna and retreated a step for the girl's protection.

Soovin turned around. His eyes went cold when he saw me. They darted towards the gun I was holding at his chest. He glanced around and realized that he was surrounded with almost twenty fingers aching to pull the trigger that would send him straight to hell.

He clenched his jaw at me and then, looked behind. He was enraged when he saw Anna in the officer's arms. He leaped toward the officer.

I and Frank barely held him in place.

"LEAVE HER RIGHT NOW!? I WILL-"

He stopped when he saw the terrified look on Anna's face. I could feel his tensed muscles relaxing in my hands. I and Frank exchanged a quizzical look.

"Shhh...It's alright, Anna," He soothed the little girl as her frowns slowly disappeared and the corner of her lips lifted to their initial position, "We are just playing a game. These all are my friends, right Hannah?"

Soovin gave me an urgent, helpless and pleading look. Somehow, I understood him. I diverted my gaze to the little girl and then to Soovin. The way in which Anna looked at Soovin radiated pure trust and love. Maybe...Soovin wasn't lying...

I loosened my grip on his wrist and smiled at the little girl not only surprising Frank and the officers but myself as well.

"Yes, Anna. We are just taking him for some work. Will you wait for him like a good girl?" I said in a sweet and soft voice.

She giggled and said, "Of course! Soovin, come quickly! I have to show you my new drawings!"

Soovin bent and gently pulled her cheek, "Of course, sweetheart! I will be back before you know it, okay?"

I nodded at the officer holding Anna who understood my gesture. He and Anna would be driving toward the headquarters instead of her uncle's house. The headquarters had a special children's room with toys that would keep Anna occupied.

Soovin turned toward me and stared into my eyes.

Then, the impossible happened. *Soovin Cooper* held out his hands. I tried to read his face while handcuffing him but didn't find anything. This had to be a trick, right? Was he really surrendering with such ease?

I whispered loud enough for only us to hear, "We both know that you can make your escape from here. You can easily overpower us and leave...Soovin...Why...?"

He whispered his reply, "I already told you Hannah, didn't I?"

He glanced toward Anna and said, "She doesn't need to see any bloodshed"

His words surprised me but what he said next made my jaw drop.

"Thank you...for playing along and...not destroying my relationship with her. Now you will take me or...?"

Still staring at him in disbelief, I walked him toward the jeep. I decided to be in the same vehicle as him because I didn't want him to pull any stunts and escape now that Anna wasn't there, bounding him and preventing him from clashing with officers.

I and Soovin never broke eye contact for the entire half an hour-long ride. We were communicating in our own silent way. His silence and body language were answering more questions than his mouth ever had.

Without uttering a single word, an entire conversation happened between us. A plan was formed.

Soon, we admitted him to the interrogation room.

As Frank wasn't familiar with how ugly some interrogations can get, I convinced him to monitor everything from the observation room rather than accompanying me. Even though I knew if Frank knew about it, he would only support my plan but I didn't want him to be involved in any more danger. He had had enough.

I took a deep breath and entered the room.

Soovin's aura had changed again. Once more, he had successfully masked himself.

There was the criminal mastermind sitting casually in the chair as if the handcuffs were just a minor inconvenience.

I stared at him as if trying to burn his picture into my mind for no apparent reason.

He smiled when I advanced toward him and got up, offering me his hand to shake. I accepted it despite knowing his intentions. Our silent chat had been of great significance for both of us.

In a swift move, he rotated his hands and with a blink of an eye, the handcuffs were on my wrists.

"I told you I didn't have any time for jail," He said in a soft voice, with a smirk.

We both had to act professionally because the entire scene was being monitored by numerous high authorities. We needed to pretend that we were just an officer and a criminal, nothing more and we definitely didn't have any silent conversations in the jeep.

"I knew you would try something like this since Anna is no longer here," I said, giving a hard edge to my voice.

I used his move against him with modifications so that the handcuffs were back in place.

We both knew we were just messing with each other. We were looking for a way to communicate with each other without the cameras catching a word. But till then, we had to continue the act.

He sat back along with me.

"We both know you could have easily killed the officers who came to arrest you. Still, an ace in innumerable martial arts gave up just like that? Didn't even try to fight...Why?"

"I just felt like visiting your place and meeting some competent officers like...Hannah Gorgin"

I acted surprised that he knew my name and then, pretended to gather myself, "That might be related to a little girl who was with you, isn't it Soovin?"

I saw the color drain from his face. I had hit the spot he wasn't expecting me to but the act needed to look a bit authentic.

He stared into my soul and understood my actual intentions. He let out a faint sigh of relief.

"Didn't want to cause any bloodshed in front of her? A gentleman, but a murderer nonetheless" I continued but gave him a look that voiced my actual thoughts louder than my words.

"None of your business, Hannah. Let's keep this professional" He spoke with unwavering conviction.

"I would have...If the little girl wasn't the daughter of Henry Spark. You kidnapped her right after killing her dad. Does she even know who killed her daddy?"

Henry snapped, "Ya, she does. You know what? I have changed my mind. This is no fun"

He freed his hands and threw the handcuffs on the camera, breaking it. I rushed towards the door and bolted it so that no one could enter.

"I just need answers, Soovin," I said.

"Are you really saying that you won't punish me or hand me over to the court? Does that...whatever we had in the jeep meant what I think it did?" Soovin asked.

"I have realized that...As you said, I am not like other robots working in the CIA, and...my experience, my sixth sense...has declared you not guilty..."

"Why?" He croaked.

"I can read your emotions, Soovin. The way you were playing with Anna...That night when you screamed that you wanted to change and have a second chance...Now, I know you were telling the truth...I...I believe in you"

"Thanks," The way his voice cracked broke my heart, "For trusting me..."

"Soovin, I just want to know...why?"

He sighed and began, "I was a kid when they taught me all this. Kill people for a living. I had no sense of right or wrong...but when I realized I was acting like a wheel for the wrong system, I decided to do something about it and leave all this behind...but there is no escaping your past. So, I decided to live with it. I started taking contracts only of other criminals and all was going well until..."

I could see tears in his eyes.

"Soovin," I said tenderly, "Until what?"

"A little girl showed up at my doorstep with a bag filled with one-dollar coins, her pocket money. She told me about her drunkard dad who used to beat her daily. She told me to kill *her* so that she didn't need to get home..." He wiped the tears off his face, "I decided to kill the one who actually deserved it"

Soovin was in tears again and I felt my eyes sting.

"I promised myself to leave this profession and give Anna the life she deserves," he went on, "I was about to turn over a new leaf but..."

I gulped. He was more emotional than I had anticipated. I could see in his eyes that he was trying his best to change. His soul was as pure as the driven snow, no matter what his past said.

A comfortable silence settled between us.

My head was swimming with flashbacks of the park, the kidnapping, and that night when he asked me for help. Now, I was seeing every incident in a completely different way.

I made my decision.

"There is an opening to an AC vent, leading outside. Anna is ten, they can't hold her here for long without her guardian. They would have to send her to Henry's brother and his house doesn't have much security"

Soovin looked at me, stunned by my statement. A smile crept upon his lips as he proceeded towards the vent. The knocks on the door were getting urgent and more vital. The officers were about to break the door down soon.

He looked back and asked uncertainly as a tint of red spread in his cheeks, "Just an offer...Hannah...Will you join us?"

I looked into his soft green eyes which were shining with anticipation, and knew what I was going to choose but I had something to do before that.

***When the door was finally broken down by the officers, neither Officer Hannah Gorgin nor assassin Soovin Cooper was found. They had left only a letter behind in Hannah Gorgin's writing, a letter requesting the authorities to allow her brother to take over her position in the CIA after completing his necessary training, due to all the contribution he had made in this case.***

# 5 Years Later

Soovin walked in with Anna on his shoulders. I smiled at seeing both of them.

"Hey, there Han!" Soovin greeted with his typical excitement as he put Anna down.

"Ya, my private investigations are going great, Frank" I continued to talk on the phone as we shared a hug and he pressed a light kiss to my forehead.

"Tell Mom I am coming to visit her soon," I said into my phone.

Anna screamed in delight, "GRANDMA!"

We roared in laughter.

Soovin took the phone from me without any warning. I groaned and punched his arm playfully.

"Frank! What's up, man?" He talked while rubbing his arm where I had landed my punch and giving me his hurt puppy eyes, "No, your sister still wants me dead. Treats me like a goddamn punching bag!"

I rolled my eyes at him as he put an arm around my shoulder, continuing his talk, "You are after *her?!* I mean...we have worked together when I was...you know?"

I raised my eyebrows at him.

He looked toward me and said, "What? Han, she was like a sister to me. Anyways, I was saying, I can give you her undercover base's address if you want...Sure, I will send it to you, my man"

Suddenly, the bell rang.

I disentangled myself from Soovin's embrace and approached the door.

I swung it open but my eyes found nothing. It was then, I glanced down and saw a package with a note written in...blood...?

I instinctively backed away and bumped into Soovin. He put a hand on my shoulder firmly, trying to reassure me but I could see the panic behind his emerald green eyes.

He advanced toward the package. I grasped his shirt, terrified of the turns this package might force our life to take. He gave me a reassuring look once more.

Together, we unfolded the note that was bedecked with blood stains.

My eyes widened as I read it. I clutched Soovin's hand tightly and could feel my nails digging into his skin but I didn't dare loosen my grip by the slightest, I was too terrified to. The note sent a shiver down my spine and I started trembling with fright. The note had a similar impact on Soovin. Although he did not explicitly reveal the extent of his emotions to me, I knew he was just as much frightened deep down.

We were frozen, rooted in the spot as the note flew away leaving a petrifying impact on both of us, that would probably last a lifetime.

*My back-stabbing brother and the officer who put me behind bars together, that too with a little daughter. How sweet is that?*

*Wouldn't it be such a shame if something were to happen to this cute, little, happy family?*

*I give you my warm greetings.*

*~ GG*

*(GruesomeGhoul, in case you forgot me, buddy)*

"*Stay tuned for the sequel...*

*- DrishKing*

*(Author)*"

# About The Author

DrishKing or Drishti Ummat is a high schooler with a burning passion for writing books. She is a true bookworm, always trying to read as many books as possible. Somehow, that high schooler got interested in writing books. Her love for writing fuels her self-publishing. She is an introvert who despises reality and lives in her own world, which is filled with horrors, mystery, and humor.

Although not published, she has written quite a few books and is slowly editing and publishing them as e-books, paperbacks, hardcovers, and everything else you can ask for.

She currently lives with her family in Bathinda, Punjab.

The author can be contacted via -

E-mail: drishtiummat@gmail.com

# Books By The Author

## The White Face Man: Horrors Of A Mirror

*What will you do when you don't see your reflection in the mirror and are instead presented with a heart-stopping murder that will give you never-ending nightmares? Moreover, it ends with a message written in blood - 'YOU ARE NEXT'*

*The White Face Man isn't the devourer of just one soul. His victims push others into this whirlpool in hopes of escaping but The White Face Man shows no mercy and slaughters everyone.*

*"I am Cari Hallen, one of his victims. I remember thinking I had escaped as well This is my encounter with The White Face man. Lucky are the ones who haven't witnessed his horrors. Beware, now, whenever you see a mirror, you will recall a white mask and a blood-stained knife."*

*But can an emotionless being like The White Face Man be humane too? After all a villain is just a victim whose story hasn't been told, right?*

## Midnight Poetry: Dark Poems With Concealed Motivation

*Life isn't a bed of roses but more like a Ferris wheel. Ups and downs are an inevitable part of life. At times, one might ask himself why he should get up after a fall when all that is waiting for him is misery and more obstacles to face. At those times, he needs to get up and stand as strong as a mountain, ready to embrace the upcoming difficulties like a warrior.*

*This poem collection having fifty hand-picked poems explores the dark thoughts one might get in such hard times and help him to get up after every blow of life. These dark poems with concealed motivation enlighten issues that you might relate to or might be suffering through. Relating to a piece of writing and getting a sense of being understood when you think that you are the only one suffering can do wonders on a mind drowning in negativity.*

*'Not too many things feel greater than being understood'*

*And a poem is a thing that can be enjoyed by multiple people with different likings. From an old person to a little kid, we all enjoy reciting poems.*

## The Curse Of KV-62: Provoking The Boy King

*This is the story of -*
*A troubled past and a lethal curse,*
*A burning passion for tombs and a thousand little secrets,*
*Hunger for answers and an impossible mystery to solve,*
*Courage to break a centuries-old curse and a promise to keep with the last breath*

*A renowned archaeologist and Egyptologist, Ken Hudson, the tomb of Tutankhamun or KV-62, and the curse of the boy king.*

*After seven years of research on tombs, Ken Hudson finally got the opportunity to scrutinize the tomb of Tutankhamun, or KV 62 with his friend Clark Limberdon. He has already lost his father to the same tomb but has plucked up the courage to unveil the mystery behind his father's demise and the tomb's rumored curse.*

*However, when he comes across a spine-chilling, dark, prophetic note written by his father for him about the tomb, his objectives change. Now, instead of just finding the secret room in KV 62 he has been given the responsibility to uncover, he is going to cross the line and provoke the ancient forces.*

*Little did he know that The Tomb Of Tutankhamun was ready to take another life with it.*

*Join Ken Hudson in his magical adventure in The Tomb Of Tutankhamun, fighting the curse of KV-62.*

## Detective Wilbur Horace: A Case That Changed His Life

*Detective Wilbur Horace - a detective with a little secret- is caught between three murders. The killer is overconfident for a reason, he is a true mastermind. Words like genius define him. He is leaving behind hints in the form of notes for the detective to catch up with his intelligence. But Wilbur Horace is a mastermind himself and he is the only one who can match the intelligence of the killer.*

*In fact, he is similar to the killer in countless ways, with similar habits, similar styles, and even the same blood group.*

*Will Wilbur be able to uncover the mystery behind the killings while hiding his little secret...? Will the killer get away with all the three murders he has committed? Or will Wilbur be able to decode the clues left behind, and put him behind bars? Or will this case take an unexpected turn so that neither of that happens, both of them lose and both of them somehow win in this face-off...?*

*Join Detective Wilbur on this case to find out...*

## A True Mastermind-JJ: What Happens When An Author Has To Save Not A Character's Life But Her Own?

*It had been really easy to put my book's characters into lethal situations and take risks that could either end their lives or save them, but trust me, it's a lot more difficult to make such decisions when life at sake isn't of a fictional character, but yours.*

*I am a successful crime-fiction author, Jamie Jennifer or JJ, as I am usually called. I lead a pretty normal life. My biggest problem can be a deadline for work but nothing more serious until a psycho killer kidnaps me and wants to kill me in front of my fans, apparently to get 'famous'.*

*I have to use my mind, which has developed a lot by writing crime fiction, to get out of his range, that too alive.*

*Join me on this life-changing adventure of mine...*

www.ingramcontent.com/pod-product-compliance
Lightning Source LLC
LaVergne TN
LVHW091123150826
845673LV00002B/954

* 9 7 9 8 8 9 1 3 3 0 1 3 9 *